WITH SPECIAL THANKS TO LINDA CHAPMAN

First published in Great Britain in 2012 by Simon and Schuster UK Ltd
A CBS COMPANY

1 3 5 7 9 10 8 6 4 2

Simon & Schuster UK Ltd
1st Floor, 222 Gray's Inn Road
London
WC1X 8HB

Simon & Schuster Australia, Sydney

Simon & Schuster India, New Delhi

A CIP catalogue record for this book is available from the British Library.

PB ISBN: 978-0-85707-252-8
eBook ISBN: 978-0-85707-695-3

Printed and bound by CPI Group (UK) Ltd, Croydon, CR0 4YY
www.simonandschuster.co.uk
www.simonandschuster.com.au
www.spellsisters.co.uk

AMBER CASTLE

EVIE
THE SWAN SISTER

Illustrations by Mary Hall

SIMON & SCHUSTER

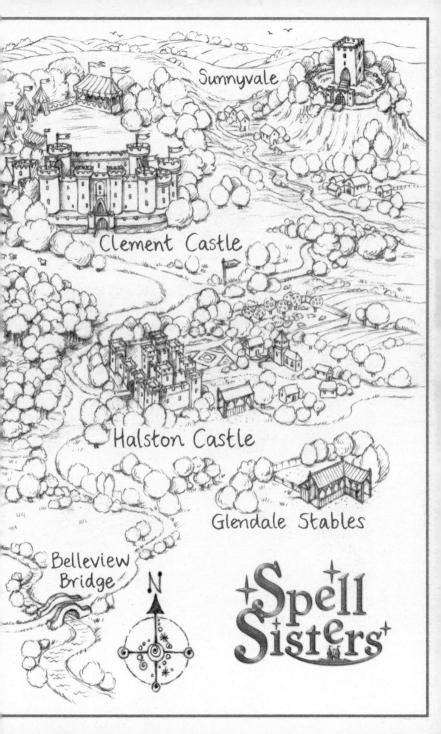

Spell Sisters

In the Forest ...

A flock of starlings wheeled through the autumn air, shrieking and chattering as they swooped and flew. Morgana Le Fay was striding through the trees beneath them. Branches cracked under her feet and the russet leaves that still clung to the branches fell as she passed.

'Those girls!' she spat, her face stormy with anger. 'They have thwarted me five times now.

I will stand for it no longer! I still have strong magic at my command!' Morgana threw one hand out towards the starlings, her fingers open wide, and then with a vicious glare she clenched her fingers once more. The silence was instant. The glossy birds fell from the skies and landed in the branches. They looked around in bewilderment, blinking their eyes and stretching their wings.

'I shall not be defeated again,' Morgana said, her voice ice-cold. 'Avalon shall be mine. If they dare try and free another Spell Sister, those meddling girls shall feel my fury.' She paused, looking around her. 'But what exactly shall I do. . .'

As she spoke, a herd of shaggy wild ponies came trotting into the clearing. They halted as they saw Morgana and backed away, their small ears flickering warily.

Morgana's eyes glittered as she stared at them. 'Of course,' she murmured. 'That will stop them!' She started to laugh, and raised her hands once more, sweeping them through the air and whispering a secret spell. The leader of the herd of ponies reared up in fear and galloped into the trees. The rest followed, their ears pinned back.

The sound of Morgana's laughter echoed after them.

A Prickly Landing

In the stables of Halston Castle, the grey pony Gwen was holding fidgeted and tossed his head.

'Why don't you ride Merrylegs today?' Gwen asked her cousin Flora, with an encouraging smile.

Flora gave the pony an uneasy look. 'He's too lively for me.'

'He isn't!' Gwen turned to the castle stableman, Jacob, who was holding a quiet bay pony nearby. 'Flora will be fine on Merrylegs, won't she, Jacob?'

'I don't know. He is a bit of a handful, Miss,' said Jacob, scratching his head. He was a tall man with a thick thatch of dark hair and bright blue eyes. 'Miss Flora might be better riding Willow like she usually does.'

Flora looked relieved. 'See?' She held her green skirt up daintily and stepped onto the mounting block.

Gwen gave her cousin a frustrated look. 'But you won't ever become a better rider if you stay on Willow all the time. She's so quiet and slow.'

'And that's just why I like her,' said Flora, with a smile, as Jacob brought the bay pony over.

Gwen sighed and vaulted on to Merrylegs,

in a much less lady-like fashion. 'Well. I like riding you, boy!' she told him, patting his warm grey neck as he tried to swing round in a circle. Gwen was a brilliant rider, and loved cantering and galloping almost as much as she loved archery.

She and Flora said goodbye to Jacob and headed out of the yard towards the horses' exercise area. Merrylegs pranced and Willow walked calmly. The late autumn sky was clear of clouds, but there was a chill in the wind and Gwen was glad of her woollen outdoor cloak and thick leather boots. Winter was starting to close in.

The castle pages were riding in the far corner of the exercise area. Gwen and Flora rode around the edge.

'I still think you should try riding a pony like Merrylegs,' Gwen said, glancing over at her cousin. 'If you learn to ride really well, we'll be able to go galloping in the forest together!'

'I don't like galloping though,' said Flora, daintily patting Willow's soft neck.

'You like galloping on Moonlight,' Gwen pointed out, with a grin.

'That's different,' Flora replied. The two girls exchanged a look. They had a secret. No one else in the castle knew, but they were involved in a magical quest. A little while ago, they had been exploring the beautiful lake in the middle of the forest near the castle. There, they had seen a silver chain caught in a rock. Flora hadn't been able to move it, but Gwen had pulled it out. Then Nineve, the mystical Lady of the

Lake, had appeared. She told them that the person who could free the necklace was needed to help the magical Spell Sisters. The sisters lived on the island of Avalon in the middle of the Lake. They had been captured by the evil sorceress, Morgana Le Fay. If all eight Spell Sisters were not returned to the island by the next lunar eclipse, then Morgana would be able to cross the lake and claim Avalon, and its magic, for her own.

Ever since then, Gwen and Flora had tried to rescue the eight missing sisters. So far, they had managed to free five of them. Three more were still imprisoned by Morgana's magic. Moonlight was the special white stallion who had helped them on their adventures. Gwen had given the horse a magic apple when they first came across him in the forest, and now he was able to gallop much faster than ordinary horses and could instinctively understand any instructions. Both Gwen and Flora loved him dearly.

'You've even jumped when you've been riding Moonlight,' Gwen went on, teasingly. 'And he's *much* bigger than Merrylegs.'

'But when I'm on Moonlight, I'm riding him with you,' Flora pointed out. 'You tell him where to go and what to do. All I have to do is hang on. It's not like riding on my own.' She glanced at Merrylegs. 'I just know I wouldn't be able to get Merrylegs to do anything I wanted.' She shivered at the thought. 'No, I'll stick to Willow.'

Gwen sighed. She loved her cousin but she did sometimes wish she was a bit bolder. Gwen knew that Flora was capable of much more than she thought.

'Look at them!' said Flora, nodding to the

pages, who were taking it in turns to gallop up and down the far side of the field. 'What are they up to?'

'Practising for tomorrow,' Gwen replied. 'There's going to be a big race around the castle moat.' She felt a flicker of jealousy. She would have loved to join in, but she could just imagine Aunt Matilda's horrified face if she suggested it! Her aunt was keen for Gwen and Flora to behave like perfect young ladies at all times.

'Will's new horse is fast,' said Flora. There were eight pages. The youngest, Tom, was eight and Will, the eldest, fourteen. Will had just bought a new horse – a dark grey stallion named Thunder. The horse looked very big and impressive next to the smaller ponies the other pages were riding.

Gwen frowned as she watched Will gallop Thunder as fast as possible. She'd watched Jacob, the stableman, riding the stallion the day before. Thunder had been calm and gentle then, but now the horse looked very upset. White sweat was foaming on his neck and flanks as Will pulled him up and then dug his spurs into the horse's sides. The stallion half-reared in protest.

'Thunder looks a bit difficult,' said Flora, impressed. 'Will's a good rider.'

Gwen huffed. 'No good rider would dig their spurs in when there's no need. Will's just making Thunder misbehave to show off. Poor horse.' Her green eyes fell on her friend Arthur who was riding a bay pony away from the group. The pony was being very obedient, doing whatever Arthur asked, with his ears pricked. 'Arthur's a much better rider than Will!' Gwen said. 'Look how happy Windfall looks with him.'

'Oooh,' Flora said, arching her eyebrows. 'So *Arthur's* the best rider is he?'

Gwen blushed hotly. She and Arthur were

good friends, and Flora was always teasing her about him.

'And if the pages were shooting with their bows and arrows, would Arthur be the best archer too? Or the best wrestler if they were wrestling?' asked Flora, her eyes glittering with mischief. But then something caught her eye. 'Goodness, what's Will doing now?' she said.

Hearing the concern in her cousin's voice, Gwen glanced back towards the pages. Thunder was now prancing and jogging as Will smacked him with a stick. Thunder plunged in protest, and Will hit him again with a determined grin. Anger surged up through Gwen. 'Stop it, Will!' she shouted, but she was too far away to be heard. Gwen clapped her heels to Merrylegs' sides and started to head towards the pages.

'Gwen, what are you doing?' Flora gasped,

trying to turn her own pony around to follow her cousin.

But Gwen didn't reply. All she could think about was stopping Will hitting poor Thunder. 'Will!' she yelled, as Merrylegs raced forwards, 'Stop doing that!'

Will looked at her as if she was an annoying bluebottle. 'What are you talking about?'

Gwen could see the other pages gathering to watch the row but she didn't care. 'You shouldn't hit a horse in that way.'

'Gwen's right, Will,' said Arthur, riding over.

Will scowled. 'Stay out of my business, you pair of milkweeds. I know how best to treat my own horse!'

Will brought his whip down on Thunder's shoulder once more, but the horse had decided he'd had enough. He was a kind-natured animal, but he was obviously fed up with being hit for no reason. Throwing his head between his knees, he bucked.

'Whoa!' Will yelled, as he sprawled on Thunder's neck. Thunder bucked once more, and Will went flying through the air, landing in a clump of thistles. 'Ow!' he yelled, clutching his breeches.

Gwen cantered Merrylegs over and took hold of Thunder's reins. 'Well done, boy,' she whispered.

The other pages whooped and laughed.

'Nice riding, Will!'

'Practising flying are you?'

'Are thistles good to lie in?'

Will pulled himself out of the thistles. 'Stupid horse!' he howled.

He strode angrily back towards Thunder, but Arthur jumped off Windfall and stopped him. 'No, Will!' he said firmly. 'You asked for that – any horse would have bucked you off. You shouldn't punish him.'

Will glared at him, but Arthur didn't back off. The two boys stared at each other. They were almost the same height now – Will was broader in the shoulders, but Arthur was strong and muscular for his age.

'Go in now, or I'll tell Sir Richard how you've been treating Thunder,' Arthur said quietly but firmly. 'You know how he feels about people mistreating horses. I don't think he'd be impressed if I told him what you had been doing today.'

Will stared at Arthur for a moment longer, and then turned on his heel and stalked off. The other pages rode after him, teasing and catcalling.

Gwen beamed at Arthur and rubbed Thunder's neck. 'Poor thing. He doesn't deserve an owner like Will. You were brilliant standing up to him like that, Arthur.'

'You were pretty good yourself,' said Arthur. 'I've never seen anyone gallop across the exercise area so fast! You should be riding in the race tomorrow.'

'Hmm, I can *really* see Aunt Matilda letting me do that!' Gwen rolled her eyes.

They shared a grin.

'I just hope Will doesn't win,' sighed Gwen.

'Well, maybe I'll be able to stop him,' said Arthur. 'My father has sent money for me to buy a charger. I'm going to visit some stables today with Jacob to see if we can find one.'

'You lucky thing!' Gwen said. There were four types of horses – ponies, packhorses, palfreys, which were ladies' horses, and chargers, which were suitable for knights. Gwen stroked Thunder's neck again. 'Maybe I should take him back to the stables? He needs washing down.' Arthur nodded, and she vaulted on Merrylegs again and led Thunder back to the stable yard, catching up with Flora who had been watching from a little way off.

Once back in the yard, they dismounted and Jacob came over. 'What's the matter?' he asked.

'Thunder bucked Will off,' Gwen told him. 'It wasn't his fault, Jacob. Will was hitting him and using his spurs.'

'Poor boy,' said Jacob patting Thunder's side. 'Young Will needs to learn how to treat horses better.'

'Would you like me to help you wash him down?' Gwen asked eagerly.

'No, Miss, I'll see to that. Cleaning-up horses isn't young ladies' work.'

Gwen was about to protest, but just then a tingling feeling around her neck stopped her.

Her hand flew to her magic necklace, safely hidden inside her cloak. She knew what the tingling feeling meant.

'Well, if you're sure, we'll be getting on our

way,' she said hastily. 'Come on, Flora.'

Flora looked at her in surprise. 'Why?'

'No reason! It's just we really should be going.' Gwen's hand clasped her pendant through her cloak. Flora noticed and her eyes widened in understanding.

'Bye, Jacob!' she said quickly. The two girls ran off across the yard. As soon as they were out of earshot, Flora grabbed Gwen's arm. 'Is the pendant glowing?'

'Yes!' Gwen exclaimed. 'I can feel it under my cloak! Nineve must be trying to talk to us.'

'Quick!' Flora pointed to a nearby hay barn. 'Let's go in there!'

The two girls raced into the dark, sweet-smelling barn and quickly closed the door behind them.

The Swan Feather

Light flooded into the barn through a small window, rays of sunlight catching the dust that danced in the air. The girls went over to the window and Gwen pulled the large blue pendant out of her cloak. It hung on a bright silver chain with five gems clustered around it – a sapphire, an emerald, an amethyst, a piece of amber and a fire agate stone. There was one gem for every sister Gwen and Flora had freed. The large blue pendant in the centre of the chain sparkled and glowed with a silvery light. As the girls stared at it, a mist passed across the surface and a picture of a beautiful young woman appeared. She had long chestnut hair held back with a pearl headband, and she looked out of the pendant directly at them. 'Guinevere! Flora!'

'Hello, Nineve! Have you found where another Spell Sister is trapped?' Gwen asked eagerly.

'Yes. It is Evie, the Swan Sister. Come to the Lake and I shall show you.'

'We'll come straight away!'

Nineve smiled. 'Thank you.'

Her image disappeared in another swirl of mist.

'Evie the Swan Sister,' Flora breathed. All

the sisters had incredible powers, but Morgana had stolen their magic for herself when she captured them. 'I wonder where she's trapped?'

Gwen looked excited. 'Let's go to the Lake and find out!'

The two girls hurried away from the castle and down the hill towards the forest. Luckily no one stopped them or asked where they were going. Shadows closed around them as they ran into the trees. The thick canopy of leaves overhead shut out the sunlight, and Gwen grabbed Flora's hand as she stumbled over a tree root.

'Careful!' Gwen gasped.

'I'm fine, I'm just always so clumsy!' exclaimed Flora. She hurried on a few paces but then slipped again on a patch of damp leaves.

She grasped a tree trunk to save herself.

'Should we call Moonlight?' Gwen suggested, with a smile. 'He'll get us to the Lake in no time.'

Flora nodded, looking relieved.

Gwen whistled, and moments later a horse's answering whinny rang out. They heard the sound of cantering hooves and then a snow-white stallion burst through the trees. His mane and tail hung in beautiful silky silver strands. He trotted over and pushed his head against Gwen's chest.

'Moonlight!' Gwen sighed happily and buried her head in his soft mane. Moonlight lifted his nose to her face and blew out softly.

'We need to get to the Lake,' Gwen told him. 'Will you take us there please?'

Moonlight whickered softly, and Gwen took hold of his mane and vaulted onto his back. Then she steered him over to a fallen log. Flora stood on it and managed to scramble up behind Gwen.

'Hold on tight,' Gwen said. Flora wrapped her arms around Gwen's waist, and off they went!

Moonlight surged forward, his mane swirling around them as he galloped through the trees. He swerved and dodged as the girls hung on, trusting that he would take them to the Lake safely.

Within minutes, Moonlight came to a stop. The silvery lake stretched out in front of them, purple mist swirled over it, hiding the island of Avalon.

They watched as Nineve, the Lady of the Lake, rose up through the waters until she seemed to be standing on its surface. Her long hair reached all the way down to her feet, and her blue and green gown glimmered. She greeted them warmly. 'Gwen! Flora! Thank you for coming so fast.'

Gwen and Flora dismounted. Nineve could not leave the water – she had cast a spell on the Lake preventing Morgana from crossing it, but it would only hold while she was in the water.

'What have you found out, Nineve?' Gwen asked, going to the edge of the Lake.

'You said the next sister is called Evie?' Flora said, following her.

'Yes, that is right. Evie the Swan Sister, whose magic controls all the birds in the kingdom. I believe she is trapped somewhere nearby. Look!'

Nineve clasped her hands and held them up high into the air. She whispered a word and then brought her hands down slowly and opened them up. A white swan feather now lay across her palms. It glimmered like a fresh pearl.

Gwen felt goosebumps prickle across her skin. She loved watching Nineve do magic.

Taking the feather, Nineve stroked it gently across the surface of the water by her feet. The water started to swirl round and round, like a mini whirlpool. Nineve touched the centre with the swan feather and suddenly the water was completely still. Gwen saw a picture appear in the surface.

'What is it?' said Flora, peering closer.

'It's a stable door,' said Gwen. It was painted red and was at the end of a row of stables.

Nineve nodded. 'I believe it must be near to where Evie is imprisoned – that's why the magic is showing it to us.'

'We've got to find it!' declared Gwen.

'But how?' Flora asked. 'It could be anywhere. There are so many stables in the kingdom.'

'I feel as if it is somewhere nearby,' said Nineve. 'But I do not know its exact location.'

Gwen's heart sank. It would take forever to check all the nearby stables! She looked at the picture, searching for any kind of clue. Her eyes fell on three horseshoes nailed to the wall of the stable block. They were arranged in a pattern,

one on top, two below. Gwen felt something tug at her memory. Stablemen often believed that horseshoes would bring good luck and keep evil spirits away, but there was something about the particular arrangement of these ones...

'It's a stud!' she realised. 'A place where horses are bred and sold. Three horseshoes in that pattern show it's a stud. There are only about three studs within a day's ride. Maybe Evie is at one of them?'

'It's worth a try! We could go and visit each of them to check,' said Flora, but then she frowned. 'But how will we do that? Young ladies don't buy horses. We can't just go and look round stud yards without it seeming strange.'

Flora was right – they needed some kind of a plan. 'Maybe you can persuade your father you need a new pony?' Gwen suggested, 'Or . . . That's it! Arthur!' she gasped.

'Arthur?' Flora echoed. 'What's he got to do with this?'

'Remember he told us that he was going to look at horses today with Jacob? We could ask if we could go with them. Jacob won't mind, and I'm sure Arthur will say yes if I ask him.'

Flora grabbed her hands. 'Oh, that's a perfect idea!'

'It does sound like a very good plan,' Nineve said warmly, but then her face grew serious. 'Still, remember to watch out for Morgana. With only three Spell Sisters left in her power, she will be more determined than ever to stop you. She is bound to be protecting every sister with her powers. Be very careful in case she attacks.'

'We will be,' Gwen promised. She knew it was no idle warning. Morgana had tried to stop their rescue attempts several times, with very dangerous results.

'Goodbye, Nineve,' said Flora. 'Hopefully we'll be back soon with Evie.'

'I hope so too.' Nineve lifted her hand in a farewell. 'May Avalon keep you safe.'

The girls watched as she slowly sank down into the water. It rippled and then she was gone, with just a single swan feather left floating on the surface.

3

The Search Begins

The girls dismounted Moonlight near the edge of the forest. 'We have to say goodbye for a while,' Gwen said, stroking him. 'We're not going to be able to take you with us on this adventure.'

Moonlight whickered unhappily. Flora patted him. 'We'll come and see you as soon as we get back.'

Gwen gave him a hug, and then she and Flora hurried up the hill to the castle.

The girls soon found Arthur in the stable yard. He and Jacob were preparing for the ride out. Arthur looked pleased when Gwen asked if she and Flora could go and look at horses too.

'Of course! You're so good with horses, Gwen. I'd love to have your opinion.'

'Oh, thank you!' she said, her eyes shining. 'Jacob, I'll help get Merrylegs and Willow tacked up.'

Ten minutes later, they all set off.

'Where are we going first?' Gwen asked.

'Hill Top Stud,' Jacob replied. 'Then on to Valley Deep, and if we still haven't found a horse we'll head on to Glendale Stables.'

They trotted around the edge of the forest. As they passed the trees, Gwen thought she saw a flash of white every now and then. *Moonlight*, she thought, he must be following them. She hoped he would keep himself hidden and not try to follow them as they rode towards Hill Top Stud.

The group crossed a ford, the ponies all jumping as a large brown trout leaped out of the water right in front of their noses. They splashed out of the ford, riding on past farmhouses where scruffy dogs barked and chickens clucked and scratched in makeshift pens, until at last the ground started to rise.

'That there is Hill Top Stud,' said Jacob, nodding to a farmyard nestled into the hillside above them. 'Bryn, the owner, has a good number of horses. He usually has more ponies and packhorses than chargers, but it might be worth stopping by and seeing what he has. He's an honest man and that can't be said of many horse dealers.'

'Perhaps there's a horse who's right for me,' said Arthur, looking excited.

Jacob gave him a wise look. 'Don't just go for beauty. Pick a horse who talks to you.'

'Talks?' Flora said, bewildered. 'What do you mean?'

Gwen thought she understood. 'A horse you just have a feeling about – that you feel understands you. That's what you mean, isn't it Jacob?'

'It is, Miss Guinevere.' He nodded. 'When you're choosing a horse you must first listen to your instincts and your heart, *then* look with your eyes and feel with your hands, and hopefully you'll not go too far wrong.'

Gwen thought of Moonlight and smiled to herself.

They reached the stable yard. There were stables on three sides. Horses and ponies were

looking over the open half doors. They whinnied
in greeting. As Gwen rode through the gateway
she saw three horseshoes nailed on the wooden
gatepost, but as she looked at the stables her
heart sank. The doors were all plain wood, not
painted red as the stable had been in the image

Nineve had shown them. The roofs were lower
and older, with green moss clinging to the grey
slates, and there were small clusters of twigs and
orange-red berries hung on every door. It didn't
look anything like the place they were searching
for. She exchanged looks with Flora and saw

the same realisation on her face. But there was nothing they could do – they just had to wait and hope that Arthur soon wanted to move on to the next stud. . .

If Gwen hadn't been so desperate to find Evie, she would really have enjoyed watching Bryn, the owner of the yard, show Arthur the two horses he had who were the right sizes to be knights' chargers. Bryn led them out one by one and let Arthur and Jacob inspect them. They checked their legs and ran their hands across the horses' shoulders, backs and flanks. Then Bryn took them down to the exercise area.

While the men and Arthur were busy, Gwen and Flora went to pat the other horses and examined the stables more closely.

'They're nothing like the stables in the picture,' Gwen said to Flora.

'I know,' Flora replied, looking worried. 'I hope Arthur doesn't choose a horse here. What will we do then? We need to go to the other stables.'

Gwen glanced at the exercise yard – neither horse looked right for Arthur. One was too old and tall and the other too slow. 'I don't think he'll be buying one here.' She frowned, 'I wonder why all these stables have berries on them though?' The berries were nailed to the outside of the doors, below where the horses' mouths could reach.

'Oh, Gwen, you should know that!' said Flora, rolling her eyes. 'They're rowan berries and they're to keep away evil, of course. Rowan protects against curses and spells. Jacob always gathers some on St Helen's Day and puts it in the tack room and up on the stable beams to stop any enchantments being cast on our stable yard.'

Gwen *had* seen some dried-up berries in the castle tack room, but she'd never thought much about them. 'I thought Jacob just hung the berries up for decoration,' she said, sheepishly.

Flora gave her an exasperated look. 'You really must try and learn about these things, Gwen. They're important!'

Gwen knew her cousin was right. She had first-hand experience that iron could ward off evil, and she had to admit that sometimes charms did work. But she did also feel that some of the old sayings and beliefs were probably made-up. 'You have to admit some of the things people say are just silly,' she said to Flora. 'Like thinking that seeing a magpie brings bad luck and so bowing if you see one? Or sleeping with a looking glass under your pillow so you'll dream of your true love? I mean, who would do that?'

Flora's cheeks blushed pink.

'You've done it, haven't you?' Gwen teased. 'Oh, Flora!'

Flora tossed her blonde plaits back. 'You can say what you like, but I believe in things like that.' She broke off some berries from the bunch they were standing next to and tucked them into the brooch on her cloak. 'I'm going to take some of these with me. They might bring us luck,' she said, with a grin.

Just then Arthur and the two men came back from the exercise area. 'Any good?' Gwen called.

'No, neither are quite right,' sighed Arthur.

'God speed and good luck with finding the horse you want!' called Bryn, as they remounted their ponies and headed on their way.

They rode back down the hill. Jacob pointed to a farmhouse nestled in the valley. 'Valley Deep,' he said. 'That's our next stop.'

Gwen looked at the cluster of farm buildings in the distance. Was Evie going to be there? *Oh please,* she prayed. *I hope so!*

Searching for Evie

The stableman at Valley Deep only had one charger at the stables, and it was too tall and stocky for Arthur. As soon as they arrived Gwen realised that their search for Evie was not over yet. The horses there were not kept in stables at all but in two large barns split into stalls.

'This is nothing like the picture Nineve showed us,' she whispered to Flora, as Jacob and

Arthur talked with the stableman.

'It looks like we're just going to have to go on farther,' said Flora. 'Oh, I hope Evie is at the next place.'

'I don't know what we're going to do if she's not' said Gwen. 'It'll be too late to travel any farther today.'

Within ten minutes they were on their way again. They had to ride through more forest to get to Glendale Stables, and Gwen was once again convinced that Moonlight was following them. She kept seeing glimpses of white moving in the trees. Merrylegs seemed to sense something too. Every so often the grey pony would prick his ears and whinny.

'What's the matter with him?' Arthur asked, riding up alongside Gwen.

'Nothing,' she said, quickly, hoping

Moonlight wouldn't whinny back and give himself away. 'Come on, let's canter!'

They urged the ponies on, cantering through the forest for several miles. Glendale Stables was just beyond the forest edge near Highgate Castle, which was perched high on a grassy knoll. The castle's impressive battlements were silhouetted against the clear blue sky in the distance. 'The stables here are some of the best in the land,' said Jacob. 'Sir Edmund is an excellent horseman and breeds fine horses. His stableman, Hugh, is a friend of mine. I have a good feeling in my bones that we'll find Master Arthur's horse here.'

The stable yard was surrounded by an orchard, exercise area and paddocks. There were horses in every field – mares and foals, shaggy native ponies and some elegant ladies' palfreys.

'Look!' said Arthur, pointing to a field close

to the exercise area. In it were six young chargers.
They were beautiful, their bay and chestnut coats
gleaming, their chests broad and their legs strong.
They trotted to the fence, whinnying in greeting.

'Look at the one with the star!' said Arthur, pointing out a black colt with a proudly arched neck. 'I like him. What do you think, Gwen?'

Gwen was so busy trying to see what the stables were like that she didn't hear.

'Gwen, what do you think?' Arthur repeated.

She jumped guiltily. 'Um. . . ' She noticed the colts he was pointing at. 'Yes, they're all nice.'

Arthur gave her a curious look. Gwen caught Flora's eye and knew her cousin understood. They desperately needed to find Evie. Had they come to the right place at last?

'Let's go and find out which colts are for sale,' said Jacob.

As they rode into the yard, both Gwen and Flora gasped. There were two rows of stables and they all had red painted doors, just like the image in the Lake! Not only that, but there were three

horseshoes nailed onto one of the stable block walls.

Gwen thoughts whirled. *This was it!* This had to be where Evie was imprisoned! She longed to leap off Merrylegs and start searching, but how could she do that without anyone getting suspicious?

Just then, a man came out from one of the stables. He was broad shouldered with dark curly hair and dancing brown eyes.

'Hugh, my friend!' Jacob greeted him.

The castle stableman's face broke into a

broad grin. 'Hello, Jacob. What brings you here to my yard?'

'We're looking for a charger for young Arthur here,' said Jacob. 'And this is Miss Flora, Sir William's daughter and her cousin, Miss Guinevere. They've come along for the ride.'

Hugh smiled at the girls. 'Very welcome they are too. I have some nice ponies and palfreys, if you care to have a look.'

'We saw some colts in the field,' Arthur said, eagerly. 'Are they for sale?'

'Aye. All those youngsters you saw were sired by Silver Wing – the boldest charger it's ever been my pleasure to care for, and as fast as a hare in flight. So was it a young horse you were looking for – one that you can train-up? Or one who's already been schooled?'

'A young one,' said Arthur. 'I want to train

him myself – learn with him.'

Hugh smiled. 'That's the right attitude to have. I wish all young knights felt the same.'

Gwen would usually have been fascinated by the conversation, but now all she could think about was Evie. Her eyes scanned the stable yard. Where was the Spell Sister hidden?

'Why don't we hitch those ponies up and take a closer look at the colts in that field?' Hugh went on. 'One minute looking at a horse is worth ten minutes of talking about it!'

They dismounted and tied-up their ponies with some water and hay. Gwen wondered quite how she and Flora could make an excuse to start looking around, when suddenly Flora spoke up.

'While you all have a look at the colts, could Gwen and I possibly have a look at the other horses in the stables?'

Hugh smiled. 'Of course. I know chargers are of no interest to young ladies like yourselves. My helper, Adam, would show you round, but he's out riding in the woods at the moment.'

'We'll be fine on our own,' Gwen said, quickly. The two men and Arthur set off. 'Good thinking!' Gwen whispered to Flora gratefully.

'Come on! Let's look round!' Flora hissed.

They ran towards the stables. The horses whickered. They were all very well cared for with glossy coats and shining eyes. Hugh was obviously a fine stableman.

Gwen patted the soft neck of a dapple-grey mare. 'I wish one of them could tell us where Evie is.'

'Maybe she's shut in one of the barns?' suggested Flora.

Gwen frowned. 'If she was, she could just

call out and get people to free her. I bet she'll be trapped somewhere no one would think of looking. Think about the other sisters – they've all been hard to find, imprisoned in wood and metal and stone. Evie could be trapped anywhere.'

They walked along the stable block, looking into every stable. Then they peered into the tack room and feed store. But everything looked completely ordinary. It was just like any other well-managed stable yard – the floors swept, the food stored in wooden barrels, the tack neatly stacked. The only difference was that there was no sign of any rowan berries – or any type of good luck charm.

'Looks like Hugh isn't superstitious,' said Gwen.

'Maybe if he had put some rowan berries up then Morgana wouldn't have been able to imprison Evie here,' pointed out Flora. 'It could be why Morgana chose these stables.'

'But where is Evie?' Gwen said, in frustration. She went over to the last stable and looked inside. It was empty. She sighed and leant

against the door. 'How are we ever going to. . .'
She broke off as a tingle ran through her.

'What is it?' Flora asked, seeing Gwen's expression change.

'I don't know. I just felt something strange.' Gwen moved away from the door and the tingling stopped. Frowning, she touched it again. Her fingers pinged as if a spark had just jumped inside them. 'Strange,' she whispered. 'This door. . .'

She touched the red paint with her hands and felt a pattern in the wood under the paint. It wasn't like the grain of the wood but a lightly carved pattern, so faint that she couldn't really see it, only feel it. She traced the lines with her fingers, thinking about the shapes they made.

'What are you doing?' Flora asked, curiously.

Gwen frowned and didn't answer. Her

fingers were moving over the surface of the door. There were long wavy lines that might be strands of hair, curved lines that might be an oval face, and a mouth open in a soundless cry.

'It's her!' she breathed.

Flora blinked. 'Evie? Where?'

'Here!' exclaimed Gwen, looking at her cousin. 'She's trapped in the stable door!'

Caught!

Flora ran over to the stable.

'Look!' Gwen said, taking her hand and tracing over the lines on the door. 'It feels like a carving, but I think it's Evie.' Flora's fingers followed the lines and she nodded, her eyes widening. 'Quick! Use the pendant to free her!' she exclaimed.

But before Gwen could take the pendant

out from under her cloak, there was the sound of hooves on the yard. They saw Arthur, Jacob and Hugh leading three horses out of the field beside the exercise area.

'Come and look at these colts, Gwen!' Arthur called, eagerly. 'What do you think of them?'

Gwen wanted to stamp in frustration. She couldn't free Evie with Arthur and the men standing there! *At least we know where Evie is now,* she comforted herself, though all she wanted to do was say the magic words and free the Spell Sister from her prison. With a sigh, she went over to them, wondering desperately when she and Flora would get a chance to use the pendant.

'These are my favourite three from the ones in the field,' Arthur said. 'I'm going to try riding them. Which do you like best?'

There was a chestnut, a bay and a black horse. They were all beautiful, but the black one particularly caught Gwen's eye. He had a glossy coat and kind, dark eyes.

'The black one. But they're all lovely,' Gwen said, and despite her frustration, she meant it. They all had strong legs and sloping shoulders that would make them very comfortable to ride. They were friendly too – nuzzling her when she went near.

Hugh and Jacob saddled up the horses. 'Right, try the bay first,' Hugh said, cheerfully. Arthur mounted and rode over to the exercise area. Gwen and Flora had no choice but to follow the men down to watch. Gwen fidgeted and glanced back at the stable door where Evie was trapped. Maybe when Arthur's riding we can sneak away again, she thought, hopefully.

Arthur rode the bay horse around the exercise area. Some of the other horses in the surrounding fields came to look curiously over the hedge. Straight away, Gwen could see that although the bay was handsome, he was slow to respond to Arthur's commands. After a few times around the exercise area, Arthur shook his head. 'He's good-natured but he's not for me I'm afraid.'

'Try the chestnut,' said Jacob.

Arthur swapped horses and rode away again. Gwen made up her mind. Surely no one would notice if she slipped away? She started backing away slowly, keeping a close eye to make sure nobody was watching her. She was almost at the stable door when suddenly she heard a familiar whinny coming from the direction of the woods.

She turned and her heart seemed to stop

for a moment. 'Oh no!' she whispered. It was Moonlight! He was being led out of the woods and down the track, towards the stable yard, by a man on a large bay horse. The beautiful white stallion was plunging and struggling, but the man held on firmly.

Gwen stared at them in shock. What had happened? How had Moonlight been captured?

'Hugh!' the rider shouted, down towards the exercise area. 'See what I have found in the forest today!'

Hugh strode past the girls to meet him. 'Goodness – a stallion! A fine-looking one too. Where did he come from, Adam?'

'He was free in the woods,' said Adam, the rider leading Moonlight, as he brought the horses to a halt. 'He seems to be wild – no saddle or bridle, and no brand. I thought the master would

be happy to add him to the stable. He'll make a grand charger.'

'Indeed he will!' Hugh said, in delight. 'He'll need some training-up though. Steady, boy!'

Seeing Gwen and Flora, Moonlight whinnied at full volume and tried to plunge towards them.

'Put him in a stable,' Hugh said, not seeming to notice.

'You can't just take a horse from the woods!' Flora exclaimed.

Hugh looked at her. 'Why not, Miss? With no saddle, bridle or brand he's ours to keep. That's the law of the land.'

'But . . . but you *can't* keep him!' Flora exclaimed, desperately. 'You just can't! A horse like that is wild and shouldn't be cooped up in a stable, and anyway he's—'

'A really beautiful horse,' Gwen said, quickly, drowning out Flora's voice before she could say anything more about Moonlight. There was no way she and Flora could let the men find out how they knew the horse, or that he was more special than they could imagine. As it was, Moonlight wasn't helping – he kept pulling towards them and whinnying.

Sorry, Moonlight, Gwen thought, feeling awful. *We'll free you later. When everyone's busy.*

'Which stable should I put him in?' asked Adam.

'Not the end one that's for sure, he's wild enough as it is,' said Hugh. 'Try the third stable in the second block.' He turned to Jacob. 'I'd give a gold coin to know what's going on with that end stable at the moment. None of the horses will go near it.'

Gwen and Flora exchanged looks. It had to be because of the magic Morgana had used to trap Evie.

Hugh slapped Moonlight on the rump. 'Put him away then, Adam.'

Adam led Moonlight off. The stallion's head hung sadly, and when he was shut in he set up a continuous whinnying.

Gwen groaned inwardly. If it wasn't enough that she and Flora had Evie to free, they now also had to rescue Moonlight too!

Arthur, meanwhile, had finished with the chestnut pony. 'I do like him, but I want to try the black,' he said to Hugh. 'He looks like he'll be very fast.'

Hugh nodded. 'His looks don't deceive. Champion's the swiftest colt in our stables.'

'Champion!' Arthur smiled. 'I like his

name.' He turned to Gwen. 'Watch me, Gwen! Tell me what you think!'

Gwen smiled weakly as Arthur mounted Champion. She wished she could be supportive

of his search for the perfect horse, but she was so worried about Evie and Moonlight, she could barely think straight.

Arthur and Champion were soon cantering around the exercise area. Arthur asked the horse to gallop and they raced across the grass, Champion's tail streaming out behind him like a silken banner. Even the horses in the surrounding paddocks lifted their heads to watch. By the time Arthur pulled him up, he was grinning broadly. 'I like him,' he said, patting Champion's neck. 'I like him a lot.' His eyes found Gwen's. 'Well?'

'He … he looks perfect for you,' she managed to say.

Luckily Arthur didn't need to hear any more than that. 'I think so too! Come on, boy, I want to try you out some more.' Arthur headed off again.

Hugh chuckled. 'That's the horse for him all right, Jacob.'

Jacob nodded. 'Aye. I think you're right.'

'There's a jugful of ale and some cheese in my cottage,' Hugh said. 'Would you care to share some with me while the young people look at the horses?'

'Gladly!' Jacob smiled.

Hugh looked at the girls. 'I haven't any drinks for young ladies I'm afraid, but I'll send Adam up to the castle to fetch you something. It'll take him a little while to get there and back though.'

'Oh, don't worry at all—' Flora began.

Gwen interrupted her. 'That would be very kind, Hugh. Thank you. My throat is rather dry.' She was already forming a plan. If Adam was at the castle and Jacob and Hugh were inside

Hugh's house, then maybe she and Flora would be able to let Moonlight out of the stable and then free Evie. Arthur was having so much fun riding Champion that he hopefully wouldn't realise what they were up to.

'I'll do that then,' said Hugh. 'Come now, Jacob. I want to hear all the news of your family and Sir William's household.'

The men set off. As soon as they were safely in Jacob's cottage, which was set back behind the stable blocks, and Adam had set off for the castle kitchens, Gwen turned to Flora. 'This is it,' she said, quickly. 'Now's our chance. Let's free Moonlight and Evie!'

Gwen and Flora raced up the yard. Moonlight banged his door in delight. 'Quiet. Boy!' Gwen soothed, not wanting Arthur to hear. Not that it looked as if he would –

he seemed totally lost in his own little world as he rode Champion.

Her fingers fumbled with the stiff bolt on the stable door. It wouldn't budge. She pulled and tugged, glancing over her shoulder nervously, but then finally, with a grating noise, it slid across. Gwen threw back the door and Moonlight instantly plunged out. He pranced around the girls, breathing on their hair in delight, nuzzling their hands and faces.

'Oh, Moonlight!' Flora said, putting her arms round his neck. 'You must be more careful!'

But Gwen knew there was no time for hugging. 'Go, boy! Go!' she urged. 'Gallop away before the men come back.' But instead of leaving, Moonlight pressed closer to her. She pushed against his shoulder, but the stallion simply pushed her back. 'Moonlight!' Gwen exclaimed.

'Go on!' She waved her arms at him but the horse tossed his head. He seemed determined not to leave. It wasn't like him not to understand.

'Moonlight, please,' Flora pleaded. 'You can't stay here.' But the stallion simply turned himself sideways to them, as if inviting them to vault on.

'No, Moonlight we're not coming with you. We can't!' Gwen said, anxiously. 'We have to stay here and rescue Evie. You need to go back to the forest on your own.'

Moonlight didn't move. Flora looked at Gwen in alarm. 'What are we going to do?'

Morgana's Spell

'Moonlight's going to get captured again if he stays here,' said Flora, urgently. 'How can we make him go back to the woods?'

Gwen looked at the expression in the horse's eyes and her heart sank. 'He's waiting for us to ride him – I can tell. He won't go unless we do. I think he wants to protect us. I could ride him to the woods and run back maybe?'

'But what about Evie? The pendant will only work for you, and we don't have a lot of time,' Flora said, looking worried.

Gwen wracked her brains. They needed to get Moonlight away from the yard as quickly as possible. '*Please*, Moonlight!' she begged. 'Gallop away. We have to stay here. We can't come with you.'

The stallion tossed his head and half-reared but he still wouldn't leave.

'If . . . if he really won't go unless someone rides him, maybe I could do it?' Flora said.

'You?' Gwen stared at her. 'But you were too scared to ride Merrylegs earlier.'

'I know,' Flora swallowed. 'And I don't really want to ride Moonlight on my own, but if it's the only way to get him out of here then

I will.' She set her jaw determinedly.

Gwen hugged her. 'Oh, Flora, you're amazing! Just tell him where you want him to go and hang on tight to his mane. He'll do just what you ask once you're riding him, I'm sure.'

'Well even if he gallops all the way to the end of the kingdom, it's better than him being captured and locked up again,' said Flora, bravely. She took hold of Moonlight's mane and bent one knee.

Gwen gave her a leg-up onto his back. Flora clutched his long mane and struggled a little to get seated, her face pale. She gingerly tucked her dress around her legs with one hand.

Moonlight nudged Gwen as if to say, 'come on, you too,' but she shook her head. 'Not this time, Moonlight. I've got to rescue Evie. Take Flora and look after her.' She kissed his face.

'Please?'

He whickered softly, as if he finally understood.

Flora gulped. 'Come on, Moonlight!' She touched his sides with her heels. 'To the forest!'

Moonlight plunged away and galloped across the stable yard, so fast he was just a white blur with Flora, clinging as tightly as she could, to his back.

Oh, please stay on, Flora! Gwen thought in alarm, as Moonlight raced up the track towards the woods. She didn't want to look away, wanting to make sure that Flora was all right, but she also knew she had no time to waste. The yard was quiet now. The only eyes on her were those of the watching horses. It was time to rescue Evie!

Gwen ran to the stable door. She realised that the sky was suddenly darkening. Grey clouds were sweeping across the blue from all directions, blocking out the sun. An icy shiver ran over Gwen's skin. The clouds were moving too fast for it to be natural. Morgana, Gwen thought with a flicker of dread. *She knows we are here. I must free Evie!* The horses in the stables started to whinny restlessly, stamping their feet.

'Quickly!' Gwen muttered to herself. She pulled the pendant from around her neck and pressed it against the wood of the stable door. She knew the spell well by now:

'Spell Sister of Avalon I now release,
Return to the island and help bring peace!'

She chanted it as fast as she could. As the last word left her lips, a shower of red sparks burst from the door frame. Gwen jumped back. The faint lines on the door became sharper and clearer, as if a person was pushing their way out. Gwen could see a tangle of long hair, an oval-shaped face and large scared eyes.

Then suddenly a shiver swept over the wood, and a girl stepped out of the door. She blinked, her long white-blonde hair swirling down almost to her ankles. There was a silver, swan-shaped pendant around her neck and she was wearing a beautiful skirt made of white swan feathers. 'I'm free!' she exclaimed, turning to Gwen with a smile.

'Yes. My name is Guinevere. I've been sent by Nineve to free you. I'm going to help you get back to Avalon.'

'Avalon!' Evie breathed, her eyes shining at the word. 'My home. Oh, I cannot wait to return.'

Gwen glanced up anxiously at the sky. The

clouds were pressing down now, a blanket of purple grey. The horses were getting louder in the stables, their whinnies growing in volume.

'We need to get away from here quickly. Morgana's up to something!' Gwen said. Just then, the horse in the next-door stall tried to jump out of his stable. Gwen pulled Evie out of the way just in time as the horse reached out for them, his teeth snapping. His ears were flattened and he looked savage – nothing like the friendly horse he had been just a little while ago.

'What's going on?' Evie said, in alarm.

'I think it must be Morgana's magic,' said Gwen, frowning as the other horses started kicking at their stable doors, staring at her. 'Their eyes,' she said, pointing. 'Look!'

'They're green!' whispered Evie. It was true.

The horses' eyes were no longer a gentle dark brown, but were glowing a sinister green colour.

'They've been enchanted!' Evie looked at Gwen in alarm. 'Morgana must be trying to stop you from rescuing me. What are we going to do?'

'Run!' Gwen shouted, grabbing Evie's hand. They ran towards the track that led to the woods. If they could just get to Flora and Moonlight, they could escape quickly. But as they hurried away, Gwen glanced at the exercise area and stopped dead.

The horses in the paddocks were whinnying in rage, galloping alongside the fences, their eyes glowing a ghostly green and fixed on Gwen. Champion was bolting around the field with Arthur still on his back. Arthur pulled at his mouth using all his strength, but the horse ignored his commands.

'Arthur!' gasped Gwen. Champion was swerving left and right. If Arthur fell off at that speed he would be badly hurt.

'Guinevere, we must go!' said Evie, tugging at her.

'I can't! My friend is in trouble.' Gwen ran down to the exercise area. Champion bolted towards her, his ears back.

'Gwen! Watch out! I can't stop!' Arthur yelled to her, pulling desperately at the metal bit in the horse's mouth.

Champion galloped past a tree with low overhanging branches. 'Grab the branches of the tree, Arthur!' Gwen shouted. 'Jump off him!'

Arthur realised instantly what she meant. As Champion passed the tree, Arthur leaped from the horse's back, his hands reaching up to grab one of the branches. Arthur swung himself away, letting the horse carry on without him. He hung there for a moment, panting hard. But just when Gwen was breathing a sigh of relief, thinking Arthur was safe, the branch snapped sending Arthur crashing to the ground. As he landed, Arthur struck his head on a tree root, crying out before lying completely still.

'Arthur!' Gwen screamed. She ran into the exercise area. But as she did so, she heard a savage whinny. Champion had wheeled around. He was staring at her, his green eyes glowing with evil magic. Gwen felt as if the world stopped for a moment, and then with a loud squeal, the black colt charged straight towards her.

7

No Way Out

The ground shook with the thunder of Champion's hooves as he bore down on Gwen once more, his mouth open, his ears flattened. Gwen felt as if she was rooted to the spot. She had never been scared of a horse before in her life, but now she was terrified, and she was completely defenceless. *What am I going to do?* she thought, as the black colt bore down on her.

Her eyes fell on the broken branch lying near Arthur. Maybe she could use that? She ran over and grabbed it, brandishing it in the air. 'Whoa!' she yelled at the horse.

To her surprise, Champion skidded abruptly to a halt. He squealed and reared up, his front hooves striking out towards her head. Gwen swept the branch at him, intent on keeping him away. 'Get back!' Arthur sat up beside her, groaning and holding his head.

Champion ran backwards, his eyes fixed fearfully on the branch. Gwen frowned. He was a tall, strong horse. Why was he so scared of a girl with a piece of wood? Champion pawed at the ground like an angry bull. Gwen swung the branch in front of her again. 'Go away! Go on! Off with you!' To her amazement, Champion took one more look at the branch, wheeled back around and then galloped away.

Gwen could hardly believe it. His eyes were still glowing green. Whatever enchantment Morgana was using hadn't worn off. So why had he run away from her like that?

'Gwen!' Evie came hurrying across the grass, her eyes wide. 'That was very brave. I thought that horse was going to kill you!'

'Me too,' gasped Gwen. 'I've no idea why he stopped and ran away.' She turned to Arthur and helped prop him up so he was leaning against the tree trunk. 'Are you all right?'

He groaned, his eyes shut.

'We need to get help for him,' Gwen said.

'And for us,' said Evie, her brow creased with worry. 'Look at those horses, Guinevere!'

The horses in the next paddock were pacing up and down, their green eyes fixed on Gwen and

Evie. The magic spell Morgana cast had affected them all. As she watched, one of them galloped straight at the fence. Gwen tensed for a moment, thinking he was going to jump it. But the fence was too high and the horse stopped at the last moment, his chest and forelegs crashing into it. Icy fingers ran across her skin. If he did that a few more times the fence would soon give way!

Gwen looked around desperately. She needed to get Arthur back to safety and get Evie back to Avalon. 'Evie, you need to get away from here. Use your magic to return to Avalon!'

Evie shook her head. 'No, I'm not going to leave you. What if the horses break the fence down? Or worse still, if Morgana herself comes? I can't leave you to face those things on your own! Not after you risked so much to rescue me.'

'Please!' Gwen couldn't bear to think of

Evie getting hurt or caught again. 'My cousin Flora's in the forest—' She broke off. 'Flora!' she whispered in sudden horror, and swung around towards the wood. What if Moonlight had been affected by Morgana's spell too?

She scanned the tree line desperately, but to her relief, she saw Flora sitting on Moonlight's back at the edge of the woodland. He was stamping a hoof in agitation and half-rearing. For a moment, Gwen had the horrible feeling that he was about to charge. But then she realised Flora was trying to urge him back towards the stables and he was resisting. She could tell the horse knew how dangerous the magic was. 'Good boy,' she whispered. 'Keep Flora safe.'

For a moment she wondered why Morgana's magic hadn't turned him wild too. Maybe it was because he was in the forest and not in the stables?

CRACK! Gwen didn't have a chance to think anymore. The top bar of the fence broke as the horses in the field continued to throw themselves against it.

Evie cried out. 'Guinevere! They're breaking down the fence!'

Gwen raised the branch in her hands once more. It had helped keep Champion back, maybe it would help now? She tried to ignore the little voice inside her saying: *But that was just one horse, how can you expect to fight off twenty or more?* Her fingers tightened, feeling the rough bark. Orange berries hung off a twig on the branch. Rowan berries! She remembered Flora tucking the same sort of berries from the first stables into her brooch for luck.

Some luck, Gwen thought, but then paused. *Unless. . .*

Her mind suddenly exploded with understanding. 'That's it!' she gasped. 'I think I know why Champion ran away from this branch!'

'Why?' asked Evie.

'It's because it's rowan wood, and rowan protects against evil. Flora told me. Maybe that's why Moonlight is all right – because Flora is wearing rowan berries and they stopped the spell working on him.'

There was another loud *CRACK!* The second bar of the fence went. The horses were almost through.

'Quick!' Gwen raced over to the rowan tree and grabbed another branch from the ground. She thrust one into Evie's hand. She was only just in time. With a final crack, the fence gave way and the horses came galloping furiously towards them.

Evie and Gwen stood either side of Arthur, holding their branches up bravely. *What if I'm wrong about the rowan?* Gwen thought with a shiver. As she and Evie waved the sticks, to their relief the horses *did* swerve away. They bucked and reared around the tree, but they wouldn't come near the girls while they were holding the branches.

'It's working!' exclaimed Gwen.

'But now what?' said Evie, anxiously, as the horses started to trot and prance around them. 'We can't stand here all day – we'll get tired. And what about your friend? He needs help.'

And what if Jacob and Hugh return and the horses attack them too? thought Gwen. She wracked her brains. What could they do? There was no way past the horses. No way to escape.

'We need to lift the enchantment completely,' said Evie, waving her branch in the face of the bay colt that Arthur had been riding earlier. The horse plunged away with a squeal.

Gwen glanced at the rowan tree beside Arthur. Its branches were heavy with berries.

'If only there was a way to attach rowan berries to all the horses – perhaps doing that would break the spell?'

Evie nodded. 'I think it would, but how can we do that? It's too dangerous to try and get near enough to the horses.'

Gwen lifted her chin. 'I'm going to try.'

'No, Guinevere!'

But it was too late. Gwen ran over to the tree and picked a sprig of berries. She dropped her stick, and reached out to grab the nearest horse. Realising Gwen was no longer holding the stick, the horse plunged at her, his mouth open and green eyes glaring. Gwen jumped back just in time. She took in a shaky breath as Evie ran over, branch still in one hand, and put her arm around Gwen's shoulders.

'That was close!' Gwen exclaimed. 'You're

right, Evie. It's too dangerous to try and get near them.' She pushed a hand through her red hair in frustration. 'This is impossible. We're never going to calm them!'

'Don't give up. We must be able to think of something,' said Evie. 'Maybe there's another way of using rowan to break the spell.'

'What sort of way?' Gwen asked.

'Well, we can't attach it to the horses, but what if we could surround the stable yard and fields with it? That might break the spell.'

Gwen stared. 'But how could we do that? We can't get past the horses, and even if we could there's not enough rowan wood here to surround the whole stable yard.'

Evie started to smile. 'That is true. But if we use my magic, we might just be able to do it.'

'Your magic?' Gwen echoed.

'Yes. Watch.' Evie carefully pulled a feather from her skirt and held it up to the sky. Then she called out in a singsong voice:

'Birds of the air, hear my plea
Spread branches from the rowan tree.
Break the curse that is cast here
Deliver us from strife and fear.'

She grabbed Gwen's hand with a determined grin. 'Now watch and see what happens!'

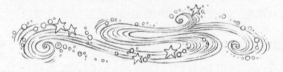

8

Flight of the Swans

The horses surrounded Gwen and Evie, their green eyes still glowing.

'Come quick, my friends.' Evie whispered, into the sky. 'Please help us before Morgana realises what we are doing.'

Just then, Gwen saw something on the horizon. It was a flock of birds flying towards the stables and paddocks! There were swans with

their enormous white wings flapping, followed by buzzards, starlings, blackbirds and sparrows. Every single type of bird in the kingdom seemed to be flying towards them.

'My friends are here!' Evie cried, in delight, as the air throbbed with the sound of beating wings.

As the birds got closer, Gwen saw that every one of them was carrying a branch of rowan or a bunch of berries in their beaks. The swans

and buzzards swooped down, placing the heavy
branches on the ground around the paddocks and
exercise area, while the smaller birds flew to the
stables and placed berries on the rooftops. They
were building a giant circle of protection, using
the rowan's magic to break Morgana's spell.

As more and more rowan was laid
down, the horses
started to slow
their pacing and
the green light
in their eyes

began to flicker. They halted, looking bewildered.

'It's working!' gasped Gwen, in delight. 'The rowan is breaking the enchantment.'

As the last few branches were put into place and the circle completed, the green light faded from the horses' eyes all together. They stamped their hooves and anxiously touched noses with each other, whickering and snorting.

'Oh, Evie, you did it. Morgana's spell is broken!' said Gwen.

Behind them, Arthur groaned and clutched his head.

The birds circled above like a giant cloud, their wings beating, their beaks opening as they whistled and sang.

'Thank you, my friends!' Evie cried to them. 'Now fly away, and take Avalon's gratitude with you!'

The birds set off across the sky. Meanwhile, the horses milled around anxiously, unsettled by being out of their field.

'Steady now, steady,' Gwen said, walking over to them. She moved confidently, knowing that horses would always seek a leader when they were upset. 'It's all right,' she soothed. 'There's nothing to be scared of now.' She rubbed their faces and scratched their necks, talking all the while. Gradually, they stopped knocking into each other and became still.

'Come on,' Gwen said, taking one of the horses by the mane. 'Let's put you back in your field.' She led the horse over to the fence. Just as she had hoped, the others all followed. One by one, they filed through the gap in the fence until they were safely back where they belonged. Gwen quickly stacked the broken wood of the fence up as best she could. She stopped Champion from trying to follow the others – he still had all his tack on, although he had broken his reins in his wild bolting. He nuzzled her, his eyes soft and brown once more. She sighed with relief and vaulted onto his back, cantering back to the others. Arthur was just starting to come around properly.

'Evie,' Gwen whispered, dismounting and pulling the Spell Sister away. 'Be careful, don't let Arthur see you. He'll ask too many questions if he sees you here. Go to the forest – my cousin Flora is there with Moonlight, our white stallion friend. Tell her everything is all right, and then use your magic to go back to the Lake. Nineve will be waiting for you. We'll come and see you all there soon.' She saw Evie open her mouth, about to protest. 'Please, Evie,' she said

If you stay, Morgana might realise what has happened here and turn up herself. She mustn't capture you again. We'll be all right now.

I'll help Arthur and sort things out. Go!'

Evie nodded, then turned and ran as fast as she could towards the trees. Gwen whirled around as she heard Arthur groan. 'What's happening?' he said, weakly.

Gwen crouched down beside him. 'Don't worry, Arthur. You're all right. You fell off Champion and banged your head.'

Arthur blinked at her groggily. 'Gwen? Who was that other girl? The lady in the white?'

'What lady in white?' Gwen said, innocently. 'There's no lady here. Just me. The knock on your head must be making you imagine things.'

Arthur gingerly got to his feet and looked around, but Evie had reached the trees and disappeared into the shadows. 'I must be going mad,' he said. 'I've got a really sore head. What exactly happened? Last thing I remember I was galloping along on Champion and he was going really fast. It felt like we were going to knock you over. Are you all right?'

'Yes, I'm fine. Something seemed to spook all the horses,' said Gwen. 'I was up at the stables.

I just saw Champion bolting with you so I came over to see if I could help. Then he ran under the branches of this tree, and you had to jump off.' Gwen paused, as she had a thought. 'And . . . and that white stallion Adam found in the forest jumped out of his stable and galloped off, clean away into the trees. The other horses were frightened too. Some of them broke the fence down.'

'And I missed all of that?' said Arthur, with a strained laugh.

'Everyone did,' said Gwen. 'I caught the loose horses just now and put them back in the field. They're fine, but we'd better go and tell Hugh and Adam what happened. The fence needs mending properly. It won't hold the horses for long. How do you feel now? Can you walk?'

'Yes, I think I'm all right. How's Champion?'

'He seems fine too,' said Gwen. 'Here, boy.' The black colt lifted his head from where he had started to graze and came over to them.

'I was really enjoying riding him,' said Arthur. 'Before he bolted!'

'Something must have spooked him badly,' said Gwen. 'I wouldn't let that put you off. I think he'll be perfect for you. And given how fast he bolted, I bet he can beat Thunder in the race tomorrow!' said Gwen. She noticed two figures coming from the stable yard. 'Oh look, here are Jacob and Hugh now.'

'Let's go and tell them what happened,' said Arthur. He stopped suddenly. 'Just a moment, Gwen. Where's Flora?'

'Oh. Um . . . She went into the forest to look for that white stallion. In fact, why don't I go and see if she's found it? Can you tell Jacob and Hugh I'll be back soon?'

'Certainly,' Arthur said.

'Thank you,' said Gwen. Leaving Arthur to take Champion in, she ran towards the trees to find Flora as fast as she could.

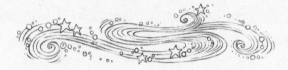

9

Back to Avalon

Gwen was out of breath by the time she reached the trees. She looked around. Where were Moonlight and Flora now? She hurried down the path, her heart thudding.

'Gwen!' she heard Flora hiss, from the left.

Gwen looked into the trees. Flora was sitting on Moonlight's back in the shadows. Evie was still with them.

Gwen gave a sigh of relief. 'I was wondering where you were,' she said.

'Evie found me and told me what happened,' Flora said. 'I saw the horses going wild and wanted to come and help, but Moonlight wouldn't let me. I'm so glad you're both all right.'

'I wanted to wait and thank you both for risking your lives to help me,' said Evie. 'I should return to Avalon now.'

'We'll follow you to the Lake on Moonlight,' said Gwen.

Evie smiled. 'I shall see you very soon then, girls.' And then, with a clap of her hands, she disappeared.

Gwen vaulted onto Moonlight's back behind Flora. 'Let's go!'

'Have we got time?' Flora said, anxiously. 'What if Jacob and Arthur come looking for us?'

'Moonlight gallops so quickly, we can get there and back in no time,' said Gwen. 'I want make sure all is well on Avalon.'

'You're right,' Flora said, and clapped her heels to Moonlight's sides. 'Come on, Moonlight. To the Lake!' she cried, confidently.

Moonlight plunged forwards.

'So you got over your fear of riding him then?' gasped Gwen, with a laugh, hanging on tightly to Flora's waist.

Flora smiled over her shoulder. 'Oh, yes. He's wonderful! Faster, boy! Faster!' She leant forwards and Moonlight went even quicker.

The trees sped by so quickly, it felt as if they had only been going for a few minutes when Moonlight came to a stop by the Lake. Nineve was waiting for them.

'You freed Evie!' she said, in delight.

'Thank you so much!'

'Did she arrive back here safely?' asked Gwen, as she and Flora slid off Moonlight's back and ran to the water's edge.

'Yes. She has just gone across the water to meet with her sisters. Come and see!' Nineve whispered a word. A silvery mist swirled across the surface of the lake, curling round the girls' boots and wrapping around their legs. Gwen and Flora had experienced Nineve's magic before, and walked out onto the surface of the Lake, treading lightly on the water as if it was the softest carpet. Nineve held out her hands. Gwen and Flora took them, and the three of them ran to where the purple mist hovered over the centre of the Lake.

The mist parted and they hurried through it until they came out the other side and saw the island of Avalon in front of them.

When the girls had first seen the island it had been barren and brown, with bare-branched apple trees and a deserted stone house set a little way up a track from the Lake. Now, with six of the Spell Sisters safely returned, it was a very different sight. The island was green again, and the trees' branches were covered with new leaves. A stream gurgled pleasantly as it wove through the orchards, and insects hummed and buzzed around the flowers on the ground. Birds sang in the trees and fluttered through the air, and Gwen noticed four swans swimming near the shoreline. The stone house was now blazing with light, and smoke was puffing from the chimney.

'Avalon's recovering!' said Gwen.

'Yes,' said Nineve, smiling. 'And it is all thanks to you two.'

'Our job isn't done though,' said Flora, seriously. 'We still have two more sisters to rescue, or Morgana will still be able to take Avalon for her own.'

'We'll rescue the final two Spell Sisters no matter how hard she tries to stop us!' Gwen said. She turned to the Lady of the Lake. 'Please find them soon, Nineve!'

'I will do my very best,' Nineve promised.

Just then, they saw Evie looking out from one of the downstairs windows of the stone house. Seeing the girls and Nineve, she waved excitedly. 'Guinevere! Flora!'

Nineve gently pushed the girls. 'Go. You know I must stay in the water.'

Gwen and Flora ran ashore. Evie came hurrying out of the house with her other five Spell Sisters – Sophia, Lily, Isabella, Anna and

Grace. They all met on the path and hugged.

'Thank you for bringing Evie back to us!' said Sophia, the Fire Sister.

'We're so happy to have her home,' Grace, the Water sister said, her eyes shining.

Evie looked down at Gwen's necklace. 'I can see each of my sisters have given you a gift already. Let me add mine.'

Plucking a single feather from her skirt, she held it between her hands and blew gently on it, then whispered a word. The girls stared as it changed into a beautiful glowing pearl. Evie held out her hands and the pearl floated into the air towards Gwen's necklace. There was a bright white flash. Gwen blinked and looked down. The pearl was now nestled in her necklace next to the sapphire.

'Wow! Thank you,' Gwen breathed.

'May it serve you well one day,' said Evie.

'Now,' said Lily. 'Will you stay and join us for a while?'

'We'd love to, but we can't,' said Gwen, aware that time was passing. 'We have to get back to the stables where our friends are waiting.'

'Go with our blessing and heartfelt thanks,' said Anna.

The sisters all hugged the girls again, and Gwen and Flora called goodbye before running back to join Nineve in the water. She smiled at them and they headed back across the Lake, the purple mist closing around the island after them.

'We'll see you soon,' Gwen said to Nineve, as they stepped out on to the rocks on the other side.

She nodded. 'I will contact you as soon as I find out where the next Spell Sister is.'

Moonlight came to meet the girls on the shoreline of the Lake, and they climbed onto his back.

'Ride safely!' cried Nineve, as he plunged away. 'May the magic of Avalon speed you on your way!'

As soon as the girls were close to the Glendale, they dismounted from Moonlight. 'You must go away from here,' Gwen told the white stallion. 'Sir Edmund's men must not catch you again. Be careful. Our task is done for today – Evie is safe now. We'll see you when our next adventure starts.'

Moonlight snorted and nodded his head. He seemed to understand.

'Goodbye, Moonlight,' said Flora, stroking his nose. 'Thank you for being so good when I rode you. You know, I think I might try riding Merrylegs now!'

Moonlight blew softly on her hair and then turned and galloped away into the trees. Gwen heaved a sigh of relief as the echo of his hoof beats faded. 'Now we'd better go and see what's been going on at the stables!' she said to Flora.

'Very well – but first you need to admit I was right about rowan!' said Flora, with a grin. 'And that learning about the old beliefs and traditions can be helpful.'

'All right!' Gwen held up her hands. 'It really did stop Morgana's spell, and if you hadn't reminded me about it, I'd never have worked out how to break the curse. Maybe some of them do work.'

'Well, actually a few are a bit silly,' said Flora. 'Sleeping with a mirror under your pillow isn't really going to make you dream about your true love!'

They laughed.

'Come on,' said Gwen. 'Jacob and Arthur will be wondering where we are.'

They ran out of the forest and saw Hugh cantering up the track towards them on one of the horses from the stables. 'Ah, Gwen, Flora. I was just coming to find you,' he said. 'Arthur told us about the white stallion getting away. Did you see any sign of him?'

'No,' said Gwen, solemnly. 'I'm afraid not.'

'I saw him gallop off,' said Flora, truthfully. 'He was going incredibly fast. He must be far away by now.'

'Hound's teeth!' exclaimed Hugh. 'The master would have been delighted with a stallion like that. Oh well, perhaps he'll head back this way sometime soon.'

'Mmm,' said Gwen, hoping that Moonlight would make sure to stay far away from Glendale Stables in future!

Hugh dismounted and they all walked back

to the stable yard together. 'Jacob's saddling your ponies. You'll be taking the black colt with you too. Arthur has decided he's the one for him.'

Gwen smiled. 'Good. I like Champion.'

'Aye. I think they'll be a good match. And I hear I owe you my thanks. Young Arthur told me how you caught the horses when they were spooked and put them back in the field. I don't know what got into them to break the fence like that, but I'm grateful to you for your help. Any time you're looking for a horse in the future, come here and I'll make sure you get a good one, young lady.'

'Thank you,' Gwen said, happily. 'I'll remember that.'

Arthur trotted over to meet them on Champion. 'Have you heard? I've bought him!'

The black colt stopped by Gwen. 'That's

wonderful. But no more galloping off, yes?' she told Champion, stroking his silky forelock.

Arthur grinned. 'I think we'll keep the galloping for race days from now on.' He patted the horse's neck. 'Come on, boy. It's time to head off to your new home.'

Gwen went to get on Merrylegs. As she did so, she spotted a white swan feather 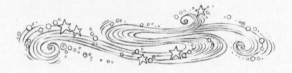 on the floor. With a smile, she picked it up and slipped it into her pocket.

10

Champion Racer

The next day, Gwen and Flora stood on the castle battlements watching as the pages raced around the outside of the moat. Although Thunder led for the first few minutes, he was tired from all the over-exercising the day before and began to slow down, even though Will smacked him with his stick. Arthur leaned low over Champion's neck and urged him on.

The black colt raced forward, easily out-galloping all the other horses and ponies.

'He's so fast!' gasped Flora.

'Come on, Arthur!' yelled Gwen, as Champion thundered across the grass, his mane and tail streaming out behind him. She half-wished she was racing on Moonlight. He would gallop around the moat in seconds!

I wonder when I'll see him again, she thought. I hope Nineve contacts us soon. . .

'Arthur's going to win easily!' gasped Flora, interrupting Gwen's thoughts. 'Oh, look, Gwen! Will's fallen off!'

Thunder had got fed up with being smacked and had bucked Will off again. The boy was sitting on the ground looking furious as his horse cantered happily after the others. Arthur was racing ahead at the front on Champion.

They galloped across the finish line, a long way ahead of everyone else.

'He won!' Gwen cried, in delight. Flora whooped and cheered.

Arthur pulled Champion to a halt and hugged him before looking up to the battlements and waving at Gwen and Flora.

Gwen waved back, grinning.

Flora giggled as Arthur was quickly surrounded by everyone else and disappeared into the crowd of people congratulating him.

'He likes you.' Flora said. 'He really likes you!'

'No, he does not,' Gwen said, quickly, blushing.

'Oh yes he does.' Flora grinned. She ran to the staircase and stopped, her eyes teasing. 'Gwen?'

'What?'

'I can always lend you a looking glass to put under your pillow if you like!' Flora giggled at Gwen's outraged expression and, laughing together, the two girls raced away down the stairs.

In a Forest Clearing

The flock of starlings shrieked as they swooped around Morgana Le Fay's head, diving at her hair with their claws and pulling at her jet-black cloak with their beaks.

'Get away from me!' she screamed, lashing out at them with her hands.

The starlings called back, cheekily, diving out of the way of her long pale fingers. They sang joyfully as they soared upwards, happy to be free.

'Silly birds!' Morgana hissed. 'If only I had stopped those girls you would still be under my control. Another Spell Sister freed. How can this have happened?' She took a breath, her eyes narrowing. 'No matter. All is not lost yet. I still have two sisters in my power, and when the spell on the Lake weakens I *will* cross to Avalon. Then those who are living there shall be very sorry indeed. Avalon shall belong to me – *me!*' She screamed the last word into the skies – both a challenge and a promise.

The leaves trembled around her as she turned and stalked furiously into her oak tree lair.

Turn over for a sneak peek of
the next SPELL SISTERS adventure!

OLIVIA
THE OTTER SISTER

Spell
Sisters

Gwen pulled on the oars of the small boat and it moved smoothly off. The river seemed alive with life. Two silver trout jumped into the air and dived back into the depths, a sleek otter swam in the shallows by the bank, its head only just poking out above the water and a dragonfly swooped in front of them, its green body glittering like a jewel. Gwen even saw a black rat whisk quickly into his hole darting by two mallard ducks that quacked near the shallow reeds. She would have really enjoyed

herself if it hadn't been for the nagging feeling inside that they really should go to the Lake and see Nineve.

'It's a beautiful day,' Arthur said.

'It is,' Flora agreed as they rounded a bend in the river and began to head towards

Belleview Bridge – a wide stone bridge that arched over the water. Its grey stones were mottled with yellow and white lichen. As they got closer, they saw Seth, one of the castle servants, sitting on the riverbank fishing with several long rods. He raised a hand in greeting.

'Hello, Seth!' Gwen called, as she rowed towards him.

'Have you caught much today?' Arthur asked.

Seth shook his head. 'I've not caught a thing.' He held up the empty metal pail beside him. 'I don't know where all the fish have gone. There don't seem to be any.'

'How strange.' said Flora.

'We saw some trout back that way,' said Arthur, pointing behind them. 'And yesterday when I was rowing there seemed to be quite a lot of fish a little way on past the bridge.'

'Maybe I should move to a different spot,' said Seth, scratching his head. 'Lady Matilda wants trout for supper tomorrow night.'

Gwen used the oars to keep the boat level with Seth as they chatted and looked round. There was something niggling at her – something about this stretch of the river didn't feel quite right. What was it? Suddenly she realised: there wasn't an animal in sight anywhere near Belleview bridge. No ducks or fish, not even a single insect skimming over the surface of the water. Looking towards the bridge, Gwen felt a flicker of unease. The shadows under it looked still and dark. She'd felt the same kind of eerie silence and stillness before – and Morgana had always been at the root of it.

'Careful, Gwen,' Arthur said, as the boat

drifted towards the bank.

Gwen came to her senses and quickly pulled an oar towards her straightening up the boat before it collided with the bank. 'Sorry!' she said, hastily.

'Are you all right?' Flora asked.

'Yes ... yes,' Gwen said. 'Just thinking about something.'

'Would you like me to take over?' offered Arthur.

Gwen hesitated and then nodded. 'Thanks.' Maybe if Arthur rowed she would have time to check all around for any other signs of strangeness.

Gwen swapped places with Arthur. The little boat bounced up and down on the water as they did so, and Flora squeaked in alarm, clutching on to the sides. But as they sat down the boat settled and Arthur started to row them towards the bridge.

'Bye, Seth!' Flora called, as they moved on.

The fisherman waved in reply.

As they got closer to the bridge, Gwen's feeling of worry deepened. The space under it looked like a dark tunnel, shadowy and with furry green moss coating the damp stones.

As they moved into the shadows, Flora shivered. 'I don't like it under here. It feels creepy,' she said.

Icy water dripped down from the underside of the bridge and dropped on Gwen's skin. She shivered too.

'Don't worry, we'll soon be out from underneath it,' said Arthur.

As he plunged the oars into the water and pulled hard, Gwen caught sight of something in the stones alongside her – it looked like the faint outline of a girl, long hair spread around her and her face a mask of fear.

'Stop!' Gwen exclaimed.

But the boat had just bobbed out into the sunshine again.

'What's the matter?' Arthur said, in surprise.

Gwen opened and shut her mouth. What could she say? 'Um . . . I liked it under the bridge. Can we go back? It was so nice to get out of this hot sun for a minute,' she gabbled.

Arthur looked as though he thought she'd gone mad. 'You want to go back under the bridge? Well, we could I suppose.

But Flora didn't seem to like it much. . .'

'I didn't like it at all! Don't be silly, Gwen. I don't want to go back under the bridge,' Flora protested. 'It's much nicer out here in the sun. I. . .'

Gwen kicked the side of her foot where Arthur couldn't see. 'I really want to go back, just for a moment,' she said to Flora, giving her a look full of meaning. 'It's so shady under the bridge, almost like it's under a spell.'

Flora's eyes widened. 'Oh!' She turned to Arthur, her tone instantly changing. 'Actually, Arthur, I think I would like to go back too. Please will you take us back into the shade for a little while longer?'

He shrugged. 'If that's where you both want to go, then of course I will.'

He rowed them back under the bridge.

Gwen's eyes searched the damp stones. Yes! There it was! The outline was faint, but knowing where to look, she could definitely make out the outline of a girl.

Flora followed Gwen's gaze. 'It's a Sister!' she cried, before quickly clapping her hand over her mouth as she realised what she'd just said.

'What?' asked Arthur, looking very confused.

'What's that about your blister, Flora?' Gwen invented wildly. 'It's hurting you? Oh, you poor thing.'

'Um, yes,' said Flora, in a strangled voice. 'It's really starting to sting.'

'I hope it feels better soon,' said Arthur, concerned. 'Now, um, how long do you two want to stay under here?' he asked, patiently, as a drip landed on his blond hair.

Gwen thought quickly. She really wanted to get out the magic pendant that she always wore around her neck and use it to free the trapped Spell Sister. But she couldn't do that with Arthur there. It was very frustrating, but she knew they would have to leave and come back later to try and rescue her.

'We can go back into the sun now,' she said, with a small sigh.

Arthur looked relieved and rowed them out from under the bridge again.

'Arthur, do you think you could take us over to the bank and leave us here?' Gwen asked him. She and Flora needed to come up with a plan. 'I think we'd better start gathering some flowers now, before we get in trouble with Aunt Matilda.'

'But what about Flora's blister? Will you be

able to get back to the castle from here?' Arthur asked.

'I'll be fine,' Flora chipped in. 'We'll just walk slowly and enjoy the sunshine. There are some lovely bluebells over there on the bank. Mother will be so pleased if we pick some of those. Thanks for the boat ride, Arthur.'

'Well, if you're quite sure,' Arthur said. He rowed over to the bank and held the boat steady for them as they got out. 'I'll head back to the castle then.'

They waved to him as he got back into the boat and rowed back under the bridge.

The second Arthur was out of ear-shot, the words burst out of Flora. 'There's a Spell Sister trapped under the bridge, Gwen!'

'I know! I can't believe Morgana imprisoned her so close to the castle. We've got to rescue her!'

said Gwen, in excitement. 'Come on!' She set off.

'Wait a minute, Gwen!'

Gwen swung round. 'I've just thought of something. What about Nineve?' Flora went on. 'We haven't heard from her. What if this is a trick of some sort by Morgana?'

The girls stared at each other. Gwen felt her excitement fade. She hadn't thought about that.

'Maybe we should go to the Lake first and see Nineve,' said Flora, cautiously.

Gwen hesitated. 'It'll take ages to get there.'

'I know, but we can't risk walking into a trap,' said Flora. 'There are only two sisters left to find. Morgana's bound to be trying to stop us. She could have just made it look like there was a sister under the bridge.'

Gwen nodded. There was a lot of sense in Flora's words, but she hated the thought of just leaving the girl trapped there. What if she was a real Spell Sister? 'Oh, if only we could speak to Nineve and find out what we should do!' she said. She pulled the pendant out from under her dress. It was a deep sparkling blue and hung on a silver chain. Next to it were six other jewels. Each of the Spell Sisters who Gwen and Flora rescued had added a jewel to the necklace upon their return to Avalon, as a way of thanking them.

Gwen looked at the pendant thoughtfully. 'Nineve has talked to us through the pendant before when we've been away from her. Maybe we can use it to talk to her?'

'That's a good idea,' said Flora. 'But how do we make it work?'

'I don't know.' Gwen admitted. She tried shaking the pendant and then tried rubbing it, but nothing happened.

'Nineve,' she whispered, to it desperately. 'Can you hear us?'

The pendant simply glinted silently in the sunlight.

Flora looked at her worriedly. 'What do we do now?'

Will Gwen and Flora be able to rescue Olivia?

Read the rest of

OLIVIA
THE OTTER SISTER

to find out!

FEED THE BIRDS!

A great way to attract more birds to your garden is by putting out some food for them. Follow the instructions below to make a simple bird-feed holder and turn your garden into the best bird restaurant in town!

What you'll need:

+ A plastic drinks bottle with a cap – you'll need to wash the bottle and remove any labels before you begin

+ A small stick (you can use one you find in your garden, or a wooden kebab skewer or similar)

+ String

+ Bird seed

+ Scissors

Remember to always be careful when you're working with scissors and glue or ask a grown-up to help you.

TOP TIPS

+ *You don't have to use food that is specifically for birds; you can use any kind of nuts, grain or seeds to fill your feeder.*

+ *Birds can take a few days to find new food, so be patient. But when they do find your feeder it might get very busy, so remember to keep it well stocked as birds can become reliant on their daily trips to your garden and will go hungry if you forget.*

HOW TO MAKE YOUR BIRD FEEDER:

1. Create two small holes (opposite to each other)
near the bottom of your bottle using your scissors.

2. Insert the stick into the bottle, so it passes
through one hole and out the other side.
This is to create a perch for the birds to sit on.

3. Use the scissors again to make a small hole
on each side of the bottle a few centimetres above
the perches. This is where the birds will get the seeds
from, so the hole needs to be big enough to allow them
to get to the food but not so big that all the seeds fall out.

4. Make a few small holes at the bottom
of the feeder to allow any rainwater to drain
away and also so air can circulate.

5. Now make a small hole on either side of
the bottle neck. Feed the string in through one
hole and out the other side and then tie a knot
at the end of the string to form a loop.

6. Take off the bottle cap and fill your feeder
with bird seed. Screw the lid back
on and hang the bottle by the
string on a tree or washing line.

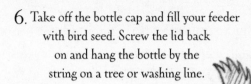

VISIT WWW.SPELLSISTERS.CO.UK AND

Plus lots of other enchanted extras!

Spell Sisters news

Explore Avalon

More about Gwen and Flora's quest

Spell Sister profiles

Activity sheets

Wallpapers

Your chance to get in touch with us

ENTER THE MAGICAL WORLD OF AVALON!

Spell Sisters